© 1985 American Greetings Corp. and CPG Products Corp.
Care Bears and Care Bear Cousins are trademarks and character designs of

© 1985 American Greetings Corp. Parker Brothers authorized user.
All Rights Reserved. Published in the United States by Parker Brothers, Division of CPG Products Corp.

Care Bears, Care Bear Cousins, Tenderheart Bear, Friend Bear, Grumpy Bear, Birthday Bear, Cheer Bear, Funshine Bear, Love-a-Lot Bear, Wish Bear, Good Luck Bear, Brave Heart Lion, Gentle Heart Lamb, Swift Heart Rabbit, Bright Heart Raccoon, Lotsa Heart Elephant, Playful Heart Monkey, Proud Heart Cat, Cozy Heart Penguin, Treat Heart Pig, Loyal Heart Dog are trademarks of American Greetings Corporation.

Library of Congress Catalog number 85-6060932   ISBN 0-910313-98-9
Manufactured in the United States of America   1 2 3 4 5 6 7 8 9 0   -01

Care Bears™

THE CARE BEARS MOVIE

Meet the Care Bear Cousins

Mr. Cherrywood ran an orphanage. Every night
he would do a trick for the children before they went
to sleep.

One night the children asked
him to tell them a story.
He agreed.

"This is a special story about a
boy named Jason, a girl named
Kim, and a group of special
friends — the Care Bears."

Kim and Jason were orphans, and they thought that no one loved them, so Secret Bear and Friend Bear went to see them to tell them not to give up caring.

Meanwhile, Tenderheart Bear was on his way to help another lonely boy, Nicholas.

Nicholas was the assistant to Mr. Fettucini, the magician at the fair. Nicholas had to work all the time, so he had no time to make friends.

One day, Nicholas was carrying an old trunk when it slipped out of his grasp and fell with a crash.

The magician scolded him and called him clumsy.

Nicholas was very sad. He wished he could make everyone understand how he felt and make them like him.

Suddenly Nicholas heard a voice that promised him that his wishes could come true. The voice came from an old book that was inside the trunk.

The book promised to help Nicholas if Nicholas would unlock its cover.

Tenderheart, who was watching Nicholas talk to the book, didn't like what he saw. He wished the other Care Bears were there to tell him what he should do about the book.

The other Care Bears, however, were trying to use
the Rainbow Rescue Beam to go to Kim and Jason.

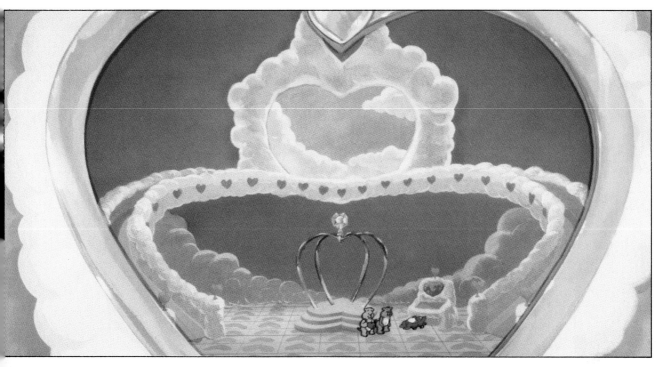

The Beam was broken, so the Care Bears didn't go to Earth. Instead, the two orphans wound up in Care-a-lot.

They agreed to stay there for a while and see if they could rediscover the good feelings that caring can give you. Kim and Jason soon began to care again. Their problems were almost over.

Nicholas's problems were just beginning, however.

For he had decided to unlock the book. It opened
with an explosion!

The first thing the book did was to help Nicholas put
Fettucini into a deep trance.

Tenderheart came out of his hiding place. "Stop, Nicholas, before it's too late," he cried.

But the book called up a mighty wind that blew Tenderheart into an empty cage and trapped him there.

Tenderheart realized he had to escape.

He used the heart on his tummy to get out of the cage. He knew he had to get back to Care-a-lot and get help.

Nicholas went out on stage and tried to perform
Fettucini's act, but he was a failure. The children in
the audience laughed at him.

"Get back at them, Nicholas," the book said. "I can show you a spell that will do it."

Soon all the children at the fair were turned into nasty brats.

Just as Tenderheart was arriving at Care-a-lot, a big wind came along and damaged the beautiful land.

"Look," said Funshine Bear after the storm had passed, "our Caring Meter has dropped two points!"

"It's the fault of the evil book that has Nicholas under its power," said Tenderheart."We've got to stop it!" Kim and Jason and two Care Bears tried once again to use the Rescue Beam to get to Nicholas.

The Beam was still broken. They disappeared from Care-a-lot, but they didn't get to the fair. None of the other Care Bears knew where they had gone.

"Let's try to use the river that flows through Care-a-lot to get to Nicholas," said Wish Bear. The other Care Bears agreed, and soon they had built a Boat Float.

Nicholas saw all of this because the evil book had given him a magic cauldron in which he could see the activities of the Care Bears.

"You must capture Kim and Jason," the book told Nicholas. Make them stop caring. Look and see where they are now."

Kim and Jason were hanging in a tree.

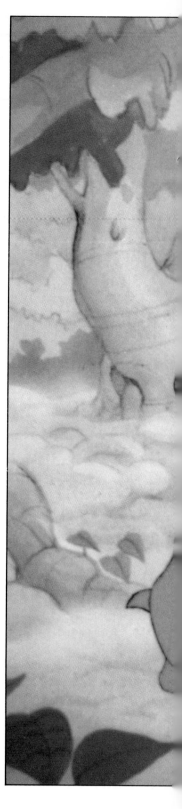

"Look, Jason, a lion is coming after us," Kim whispered.

The lion looked fierce, but it was really friendly. With the help of a playful monkey, it helped the children down from the tree.

"Where did you come from?" Jason asked.
"Nowhere," answered the lion. "We live here.
This is the Forest of Feelings. I'm Brave Heart Lion,
and this is Playful Heart Monkey. There are others of
us, too. We all want to help."

Nicholas looked into the cauldron and saw what was happening, so he made up spells to defeat the Care Bears and to capture Kim and Jason.

Nicholas's first spell turned into a big fish that tried to sink the Boat Float.

Luckily, the Boat Float had reached the edge of the Forest of Feelings.

Cozy Heart Penguin and Lotsa Heart Elephant saved the Care Bears from the huge fish.

Next the spell turned into a giant tree that tried to capture Kim and Jason as they walked through the Forest of Feelings.

Swift Heart Rabbit helped the children escape.

Then the spell became a fierce bird that chased Kim and Jason.

It appeared as if the children were in real trouble.

But just then the Boat Float appeared, and the Care Bear Stare drove the bird away.

Soon all the Care Bears had met the creatures of the Forest of Feelings. "You are so much like us that you could be our cousins," said Tenderheart Bear. "Maybe we are," Brave Heart agreed.

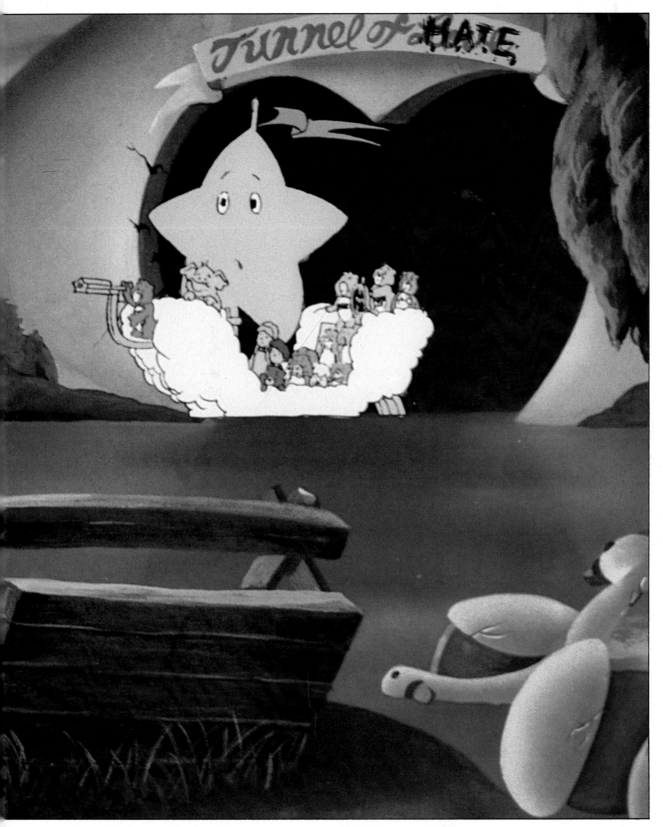

The Care Bears and the Care Bear Cousins
went quickly on their way to the fairground
to try to save Nicholas.

When they arrived, the Care Bears were sad to see that Nicholas's spells had made the fairground an ugly place.

While they were walking alone and looking at what the spells had done, Kim and Jason ran into Nicholas. He was looking for the final ingredient he needed for the spell that would make everyone in the world not care anymore.

Nicholas tried to capture Jason and Kim, but they ran into the fun house and began to get away from him.

Suddenly Nicholas stopped chasing them. He looked down and said, "I've finally found the thing I need for my spell: old, chewed bubble gum. Now I can make sure that no one will care anymore!

Tenderheart saw Nicholas going to mix the final
spell. "Care Bear Emergency!" he called. All the Care
Bears and the Care Bear Cousins joined him.

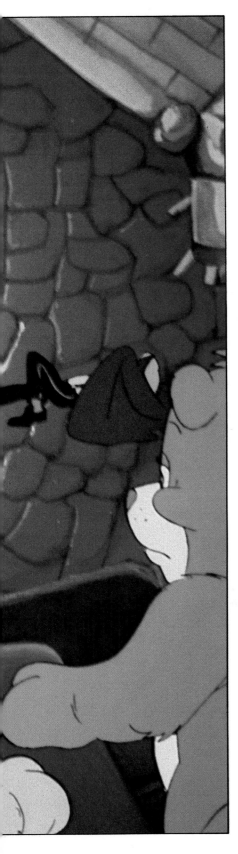

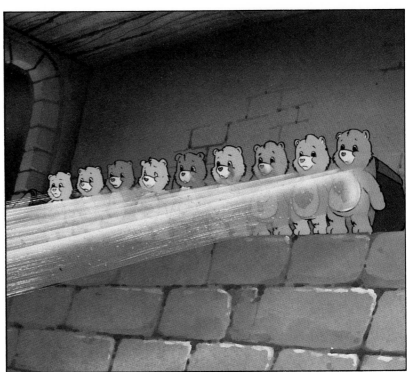

All the creatures confronted
Nicholas, and the Care Bears
gave the Care Bear stare.

It was not strong enough, so
the Care Bear Cousins gave
their Call.

Even the Call was not strong enough.
Finally Jason and Kim came forward.

"Nicholas," they said. "Stop the
spell. We care about you and want
to be your friend. Believe us."

Nicholas hesitated. "I...I do believe you," he said
at last. "No !" cried the book. "Don't listen to them.
Listen to me!"

But before it could say more, Nicholas slammed the
cover of the book shut and locked it.

Nicholas turned to Jason, Kim, the Care Bears and
the Care Bear Cousins. "Thank you for caring about
me," he said. "I love you."

When Nicholas spoke those words, wonderful things
began to happen. New life came back to the fairground.

Mr. Fettucini woke up and asked
Nicholas to be his partner in the
magic show.

And soon after that Jason and Kim found wonderful
parents. Nicholas discovered that he had learned a
great lesson. The best way to make a friend is to be a
friend yourself.

"And that," said Mr. Cherrywood to the sleepy orphans, "is the end of my story. Goodnight to you all. Sleep tight." Mr. Cherrywood quietly closed the door and walked to where his wife sat knitting.

"Nicholas," she said, "You've kept those children up very late. Whatever shall I do with you?" "Just care for me, dear," Mr. Cherrywood replied. "Then I can tell the children that Nicholas never forgot what the Care Bears taught him, and that he and his wife lived happily ever after."